GOSCINNY AND UDERZO
PRESENT
AN ASTERIX ADVENTURE

ASTERIX AND THE MAGIC CARPET

WRITTEN AND ILLUSTRATED BY UDERZO
TRANSLATED BY ANTHEA BELL AND DEREK HOCKRIDGE

HODDER AND STOUGHTON

LONDON   SYDNEY   AUCKLAND   TORONTO

British Library Cataloguing in Publication Data

Uderzo
   Asterix and the magic carpet.
   I. Title   II. Asterix chez Rahazade. *English*
843´.914 [J]   PZ7

   ISBN 0-340-40957-6
   ISBN 0-340-42720-5 pbk

Original edition © Les Editions Albert Rene, Goscinny-Uderzo, 1987
English translation © Les Editions Albert Rene, Goscinny-Uderzo, 1988
Exclusive licensee: Hodder and Stoughton Ltd
Translators: Anthea Bell and Derek Hockridge

First published in Great Britain 1988 (cased)

Published by Hodder and Stoughton Children's Books,
a division of Hodder and Stoughton Ltd,
Mill Road, Dunton Green, Sevenoaks, Kent TN13 2YJ

Printed in Belgium by Henri Proost et Cie, Turnhout

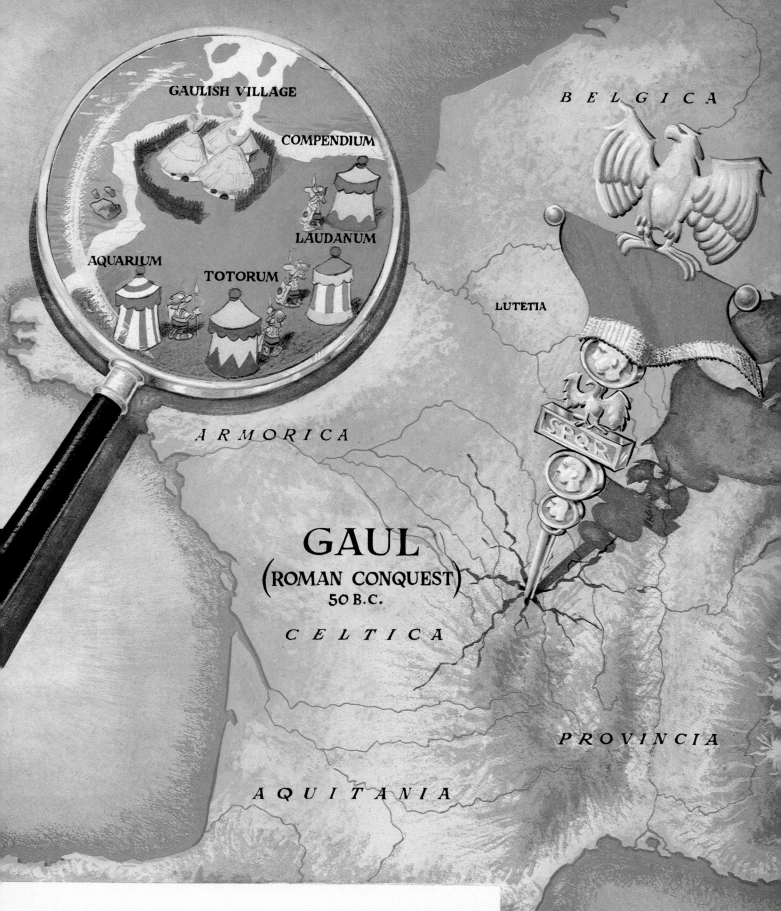

The year is 50 BC. Gaul is entirely occupied by the Romans. Well, not entirely... One small village of indomitable Gauls still holds out against the invaders. And life is not easy for the Roman legionaries who garrison the fortified camps of Totorum, Aquarium, Laudanum and Compendium...

a few of the Gauls

Asterix, the hero of these adventures. A shrewd, cunning little warrior, all perilous missions are immediately entrusted to him. Asterix gets his superhuman strength from the magic potion brewed by the druid Getafix . . .

Obelix, Asterix's inseparable friend. A menhir delivery-man by trade, addicted to wild boar. Obelix is always ready to drop everything and go off on a new adventure with Asterix – so long as there's wild boar to eat, and plenty of fighting. His constant companion is Dogmatix, the only known canine ecologist, who howls with despair when a tree is cut down.

Getafix, the venerable village druid. Gathers mistletoe and brews magic potions. His speciality is the potion which gives the drinker superhuman strength. But Getafix also has other recipes up his sleeve . . .

Cacofonix, the bard. Opinion is divided as to his musical gifts. Cacofonix thinks he's a genius. Everyone else thinks he's unspeakable. But so long as he doesn't speak, let alone sing, everybody likes him . . .

Finally, Vitalstatistix, the chief of the tribe. Majestic, brave and hot-tempered, the old warrior is respected by his men and feared by his enemies. Vitalstatistix himself has only one fear; he is afraid the sky may fall on his head tomorrow. But as he always says, 'Tomorrow never comes.'

OH, WHAT A BEAUTIFUL MORNING, OH, WHAT A BEAUTIFUL DAY... AND THE GAULS HAVE GOT A WONDERFUL FEELING EVERYTHING'S GOING THEIR WAY IN THEIR BRAND-NEW VILLAGE...

FOR AS YOU MAY REMEMBER...

THE ROMANS BURNED OUR VILLAGE TO THE GROUND*. CAESAR, ASHAMED OF WHAT THEY HAD DONE, TOLD HIS MEN TO REBUILD IT... FAIR ENOUGH, BUT THAT DOESN'T MEAN WE'RE ALL SQUARE. AND SO, DEAR FRIENDS...

*SEE ASTERIX AND SON

... I PROPOSE A TOAST TO THE REBIRTH OF THIS IMPOSING AND MAGNIFICENT SYMBOL OF OUR RESISTANCE TO THE ROMAN EMPIRE, AND IN PAYING SUITABLE TRIBUTE TO THIS, THE LAST BULWARK OF THE LIBERTIES OF OUR GREAT GAULISH NATION, I SAY TO YOU NOW...

I REALLY LIKED WATCHING THE ROMANS REBUILD OUR VILLAGE, ASTERIX!

YES, SPECIALLY WHEN THEY WERE GOING SLOW AND YOU THREW MENHIRS AT THEM TO SHOW YOU COULD STONEWALL TOO!

...I SAY TO YOU NOW...

WELL, THEY DID GET THE JOB DONE AHEAD OF SCHEDULE!

FEAR IS SOMETIMES A REMARKABLE STIMULUS, OBELIX!

HOW NICE TO HAVE BRAND-NEW HUTS TO LIVE IN!

YES, BUT I WOULDN'T HAVE MINDED A SPOT OF MODERN ARCHITECTURE WHILE THEY WERE ABOUT IT. FOR INSTANCE, VILLAS IN THE GALLO-ROMAN STYLE!

ROMAN COLUMNS ARE A TERRIBLE PRICE... SIMPLY RUINOUS!

THAT'S FUNNY... I DON'T SEEM TO SEE CACOFONIX THE BARD ANYWHERE!

8

9

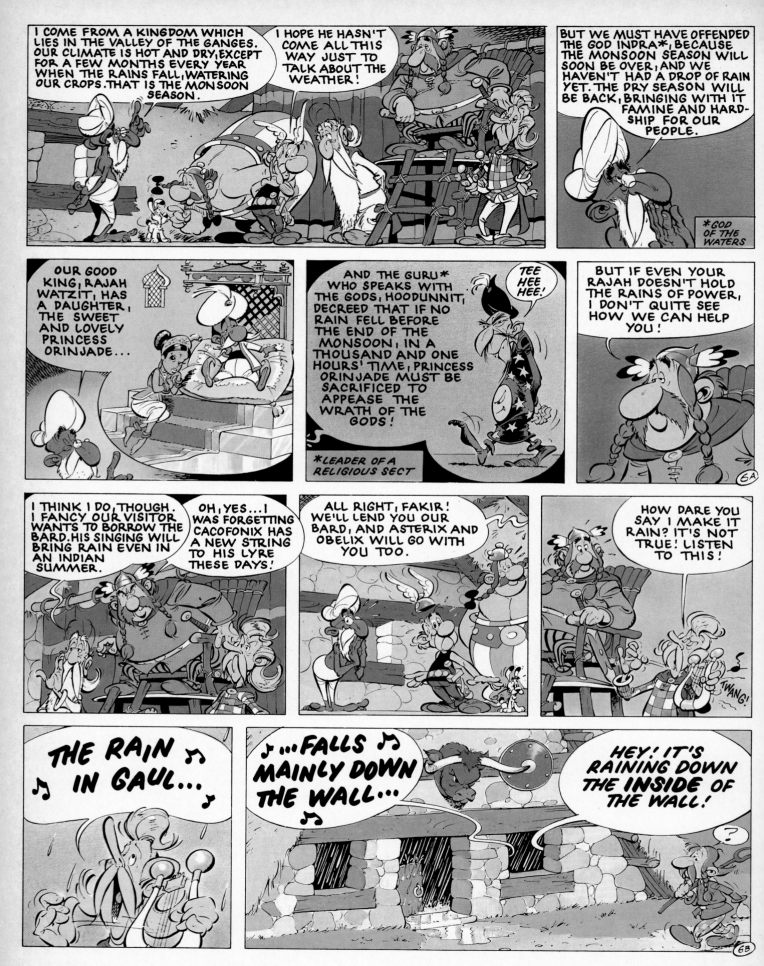

10

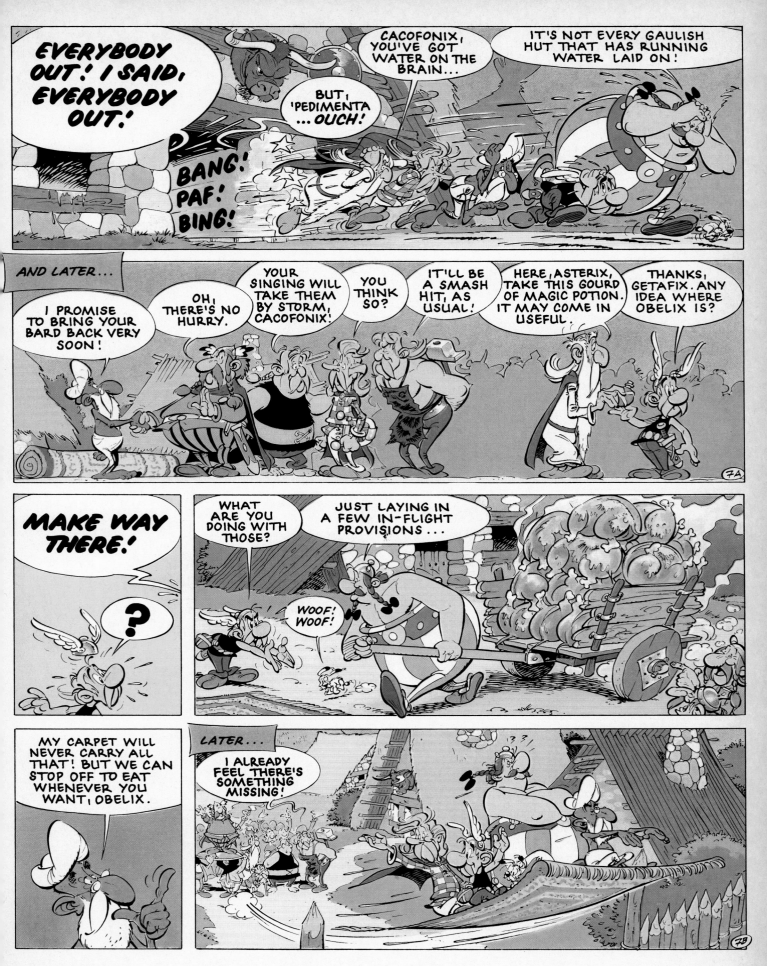

12

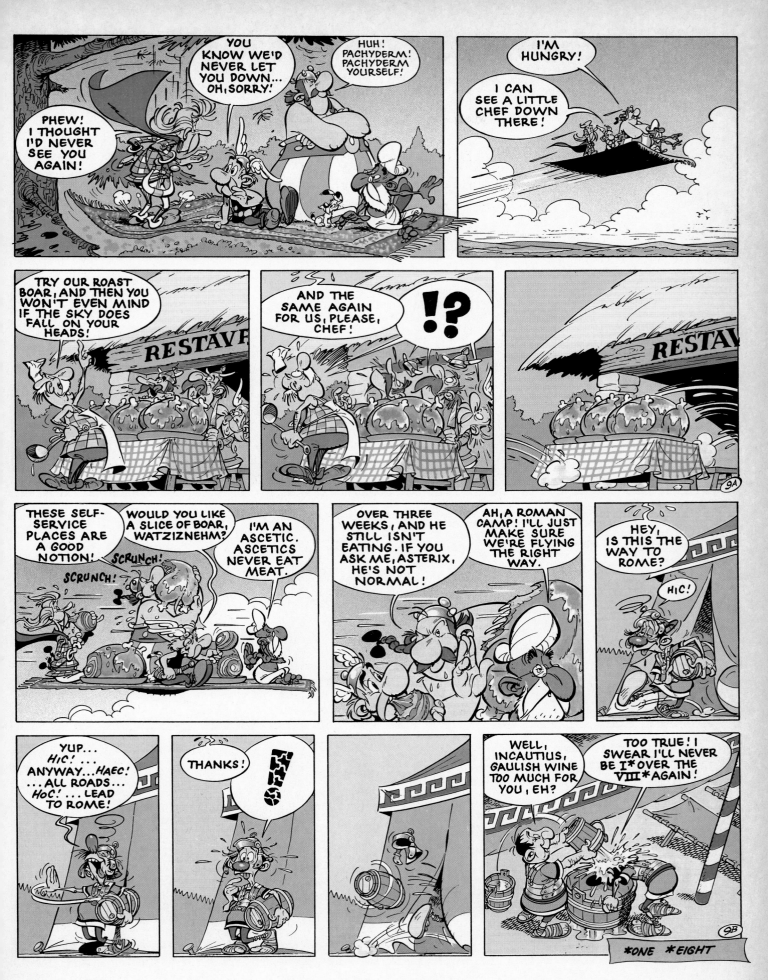

14

15

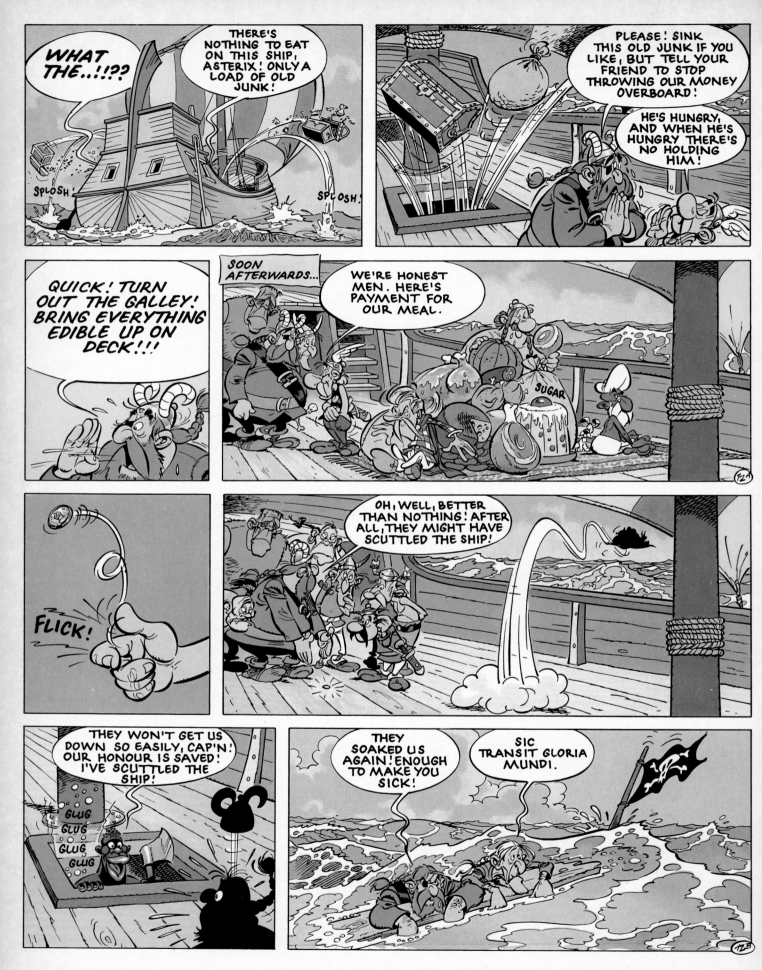

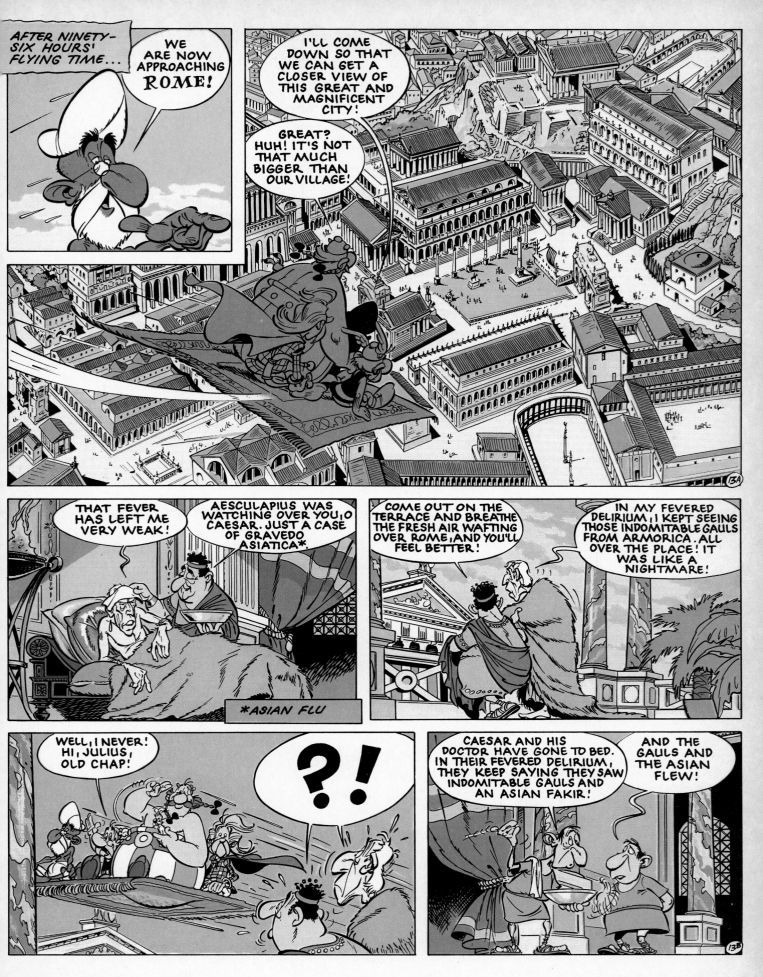

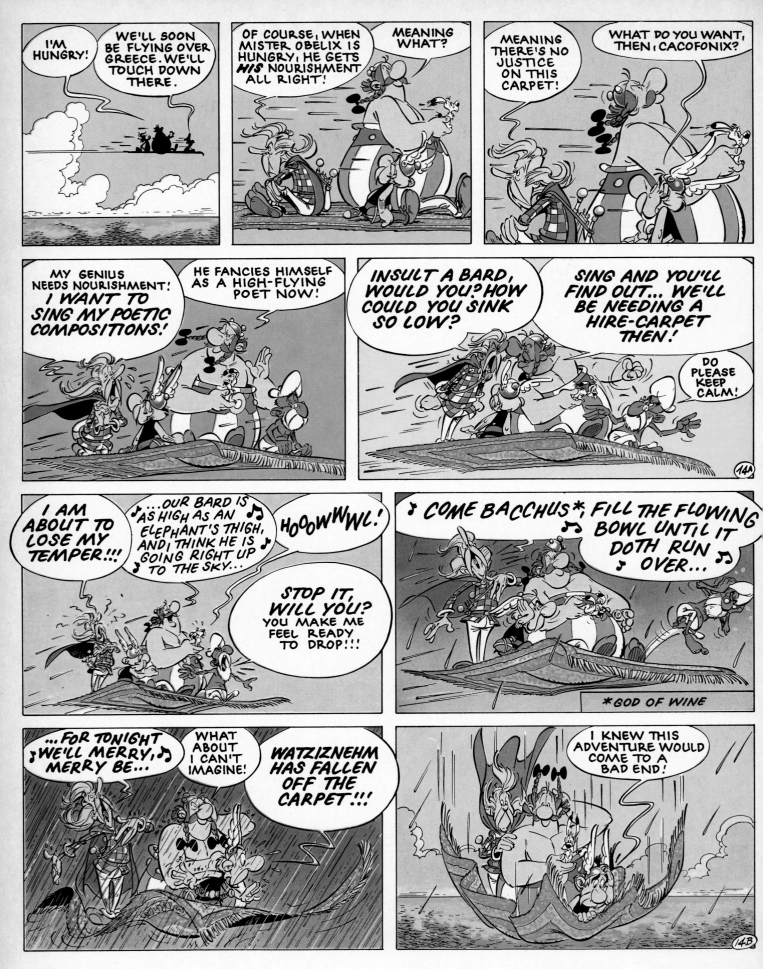

18

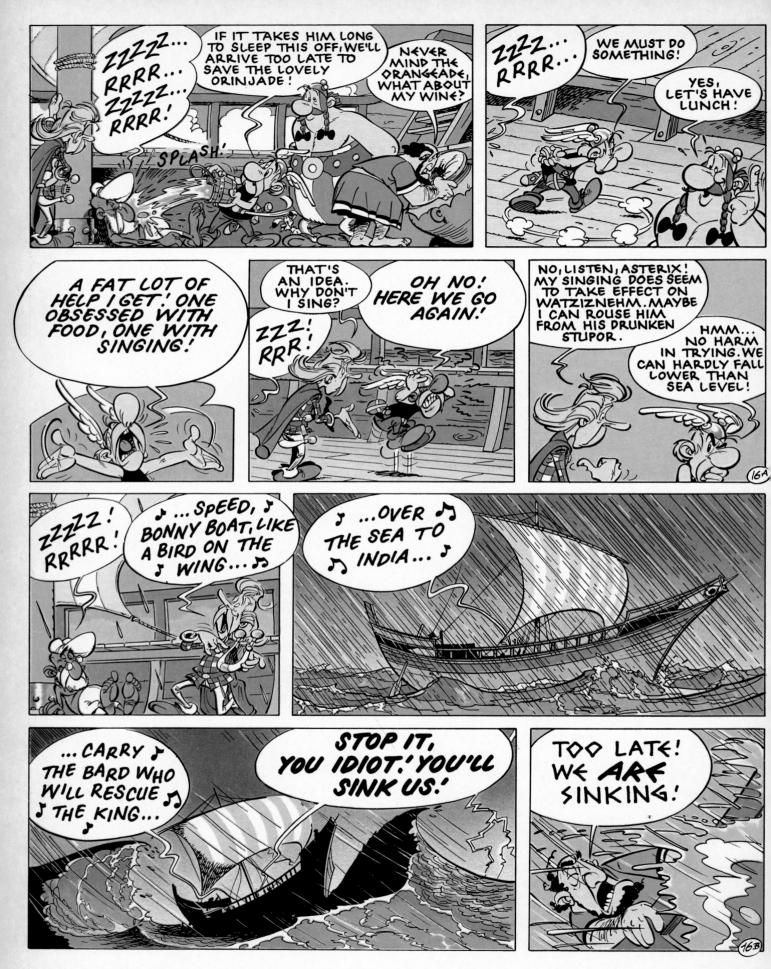

21

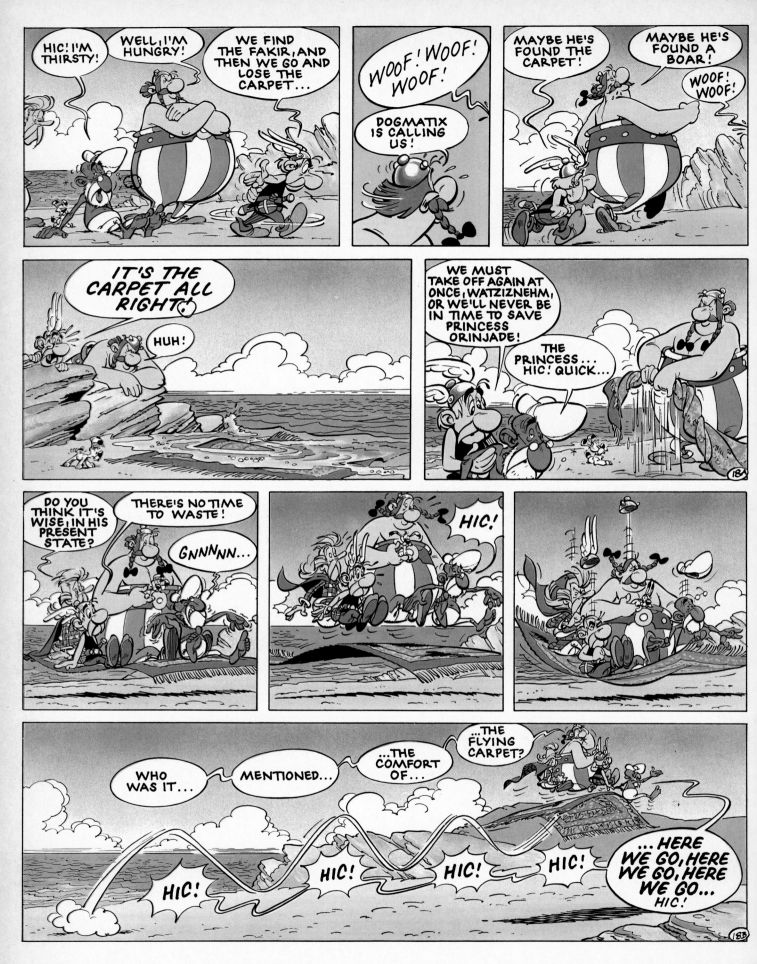

23

28

29

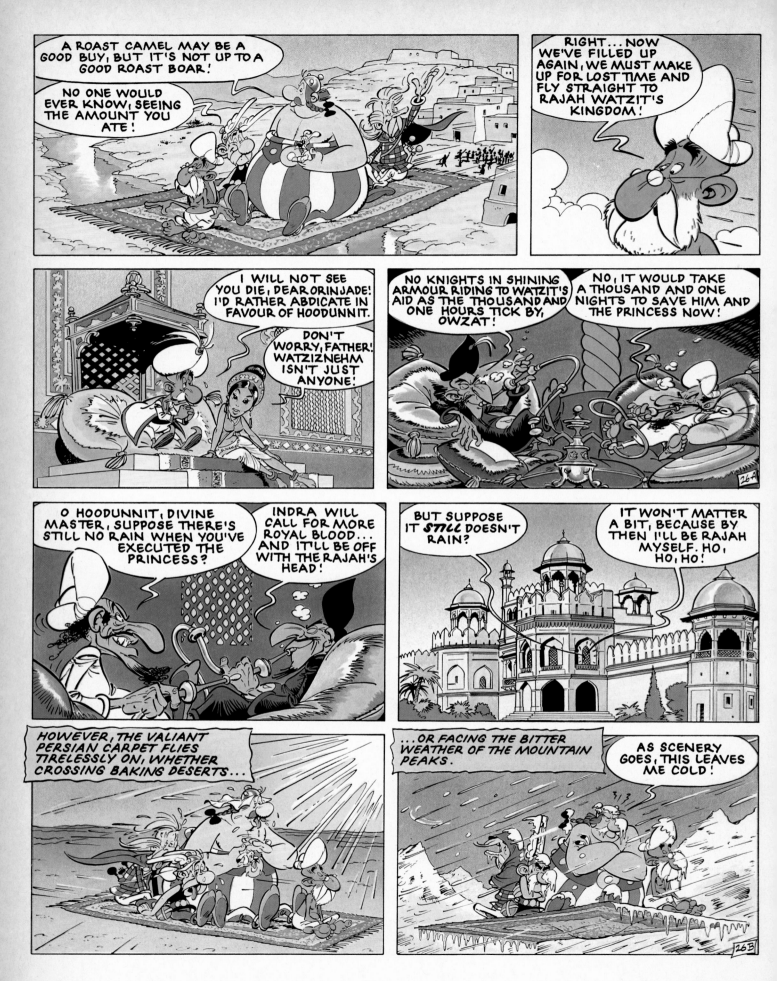

33

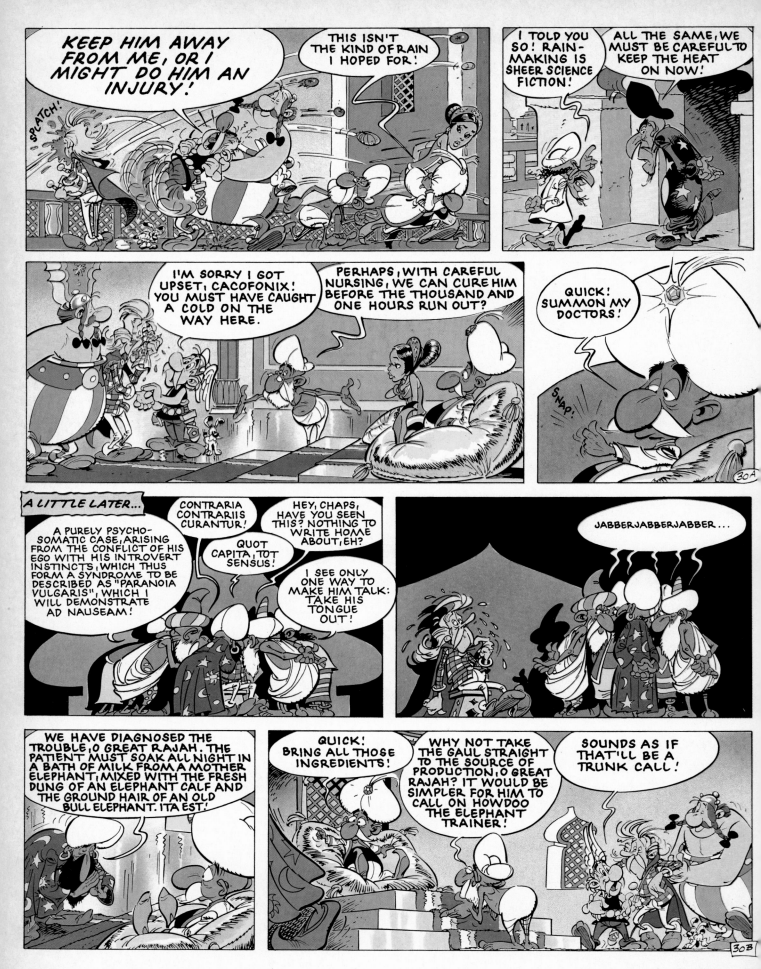

34

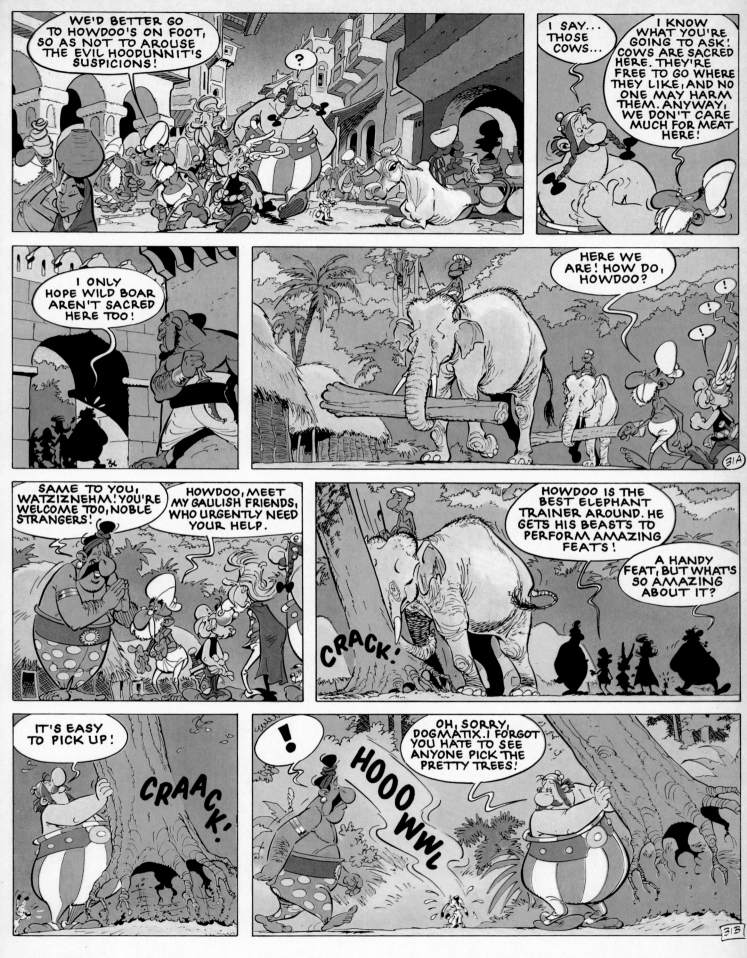

35

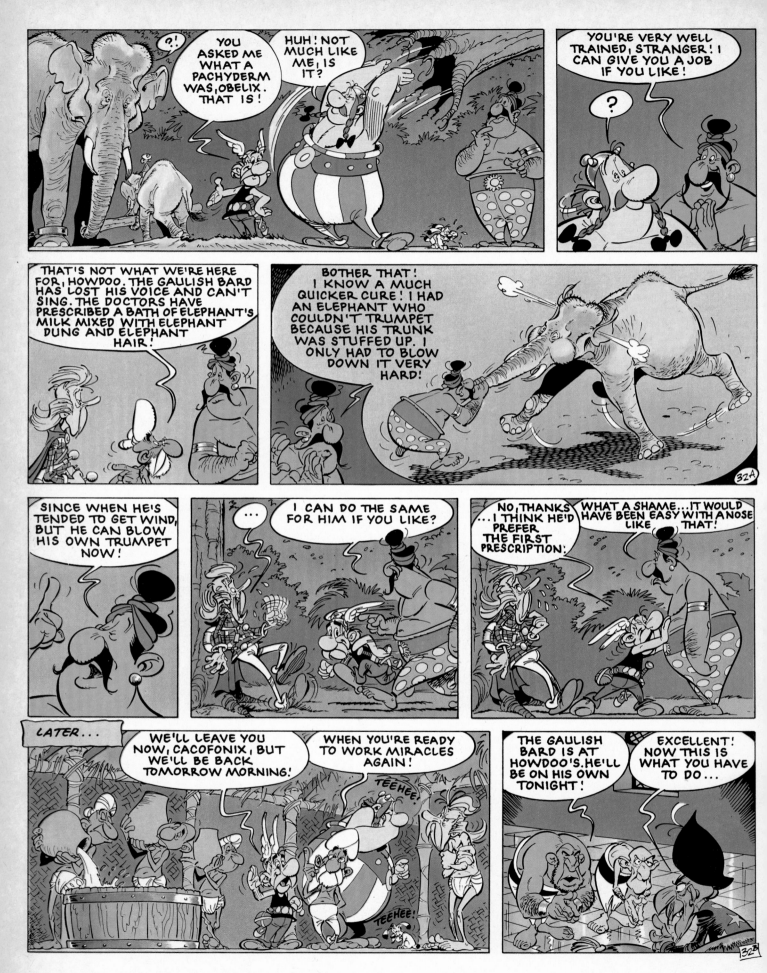

37

38

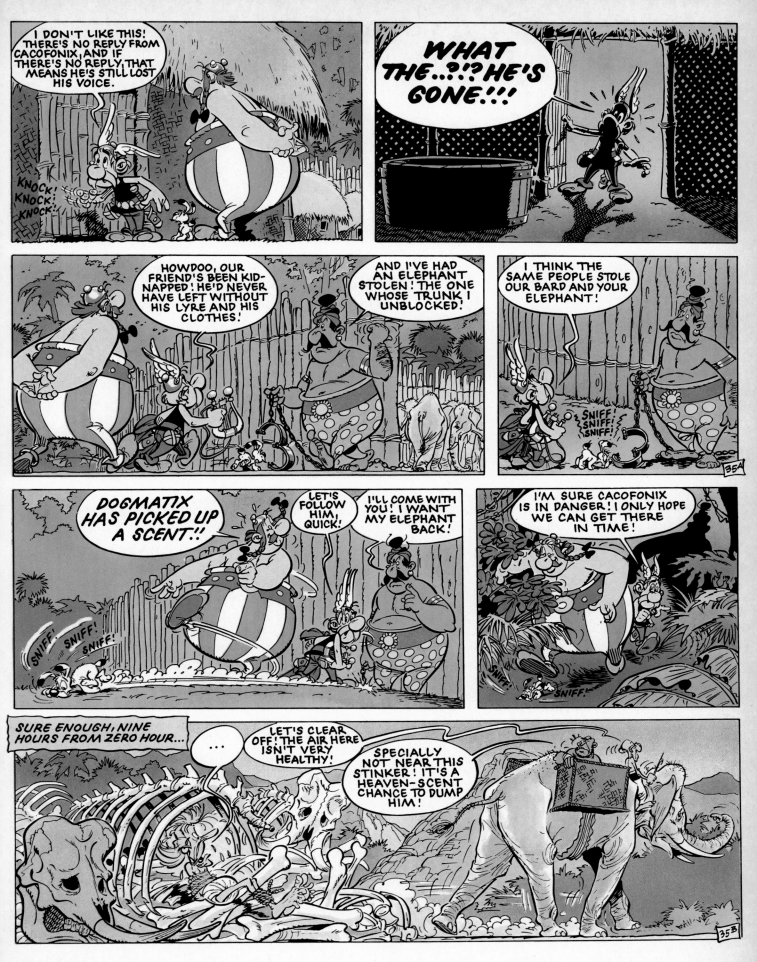

40

46